CW01064945

THE
CHAMPAK
STORY BOX

RUPA

Published by
Rupa Publications India Pvt. Ltd 2022
7/16, Ansari Road, Daryaganj
New Delhi 110002

Sales Centres:
Prayagraj Bengaluru Chennai
Hyderabad Jaipur Kathmandu
Kolkata Mumbai

P-ISBN: 978-93-5520-360-1
E-ISBN: 978-93-5520-368-7

Third impression 2023

10 9 8 7 6 5 4 3

Printed in India

TABLE OF CONTENTS

 HUMOUR

BRAVERY

FOOD

FRIENDSHIP

TRAVEL

DECISION-MAKING

KAMAKSHI'S MISSING SOCKS

By Radhika Venkatarayan

It was a very cold Monday **WINTER** morning and Kamakshi was getting ready for school. *Oh, why do Mondays come so quickly*, she thought to herself. But at least she would meet her friends again, so that was something to be happy about.

She had woken up a little late this morning. It was so difficult to wake up early in

5

winter. She had to hurry, or else she would miss the school bus. She wore her navy blue **SKIRT** and tucked in her white shirt, which was her very smart uniform. She then peeped under her bed looking for something, wildly swinging her arms and pulling out all kinds of things. She found a ball, one of those glowing bouncy ones.

She found a pencil that she thought she had lost. She even found a half-eaten **COOKIE**.

But she did not find that one thing that she was looking for. Why, why, why? When she was already getting LATE.

Always late

Just at that moment, her mother came into the room with a glass in her hand; it was Kamakshi's favourite, milk with **COCOA**.

"What are you doing, Kamster," Amma asked her looking at all the things that she had pulled out from under her bed, "Your school van will be here anytime now. Hurry up."

But Kamakshi continued to investigate looking for things **under** her bed. In fact, now she was on all fours and pulling out more things. It was missing, just as she had feared.

"Amma, I can't go to **SCHOOL** today," she finally announced. Though she loved to be at home, she also loved school. And now she felt sad.

"Why not? Did you not complete your homework?" Amma asked as she sat down next to her.

"No, I have completed all my **HOMEWORK**. I always do," Kamakshi said. "Is there some period in school today that you don't like," Amma wanted to know.

Where's her sock?

"No, Amma. I can't go to school today because I have just one sock. I can't find the other one. Everyone will **LAUGH** at me," Kamakshi said, sticking her leg out.

Holding her face in her palms, she sat there thinking about how she would miss her favourite Art and Craft period in school.

Amma put down the glass of milk by her bed and took Kamakshi into her arms. "How about we team up and try

and find your **missing** sock? Two pairs of eyes are better than one," Amma said. Kamakshi nodded her head.

The never-ending search

Kamakshi and Amma giggled as they got down on all fours and attempted to search for the missing **SOCKS**. They looked under the table and behind the chair. They looked

inside the laundry basket and inside every cupboard. They even looked inside their dog Sasha's **MOUTH!** Sasha was not happy at all with this.

Alas! The missing sock was nowhere to be seen. It had mysteriously gone missing. And just as they were going to stop their search, they heard a little noise.

They looked up and down and everywhere around, and saw that the noise seemed to be coming from the corner of the room.

In fact, the noise seemed to be coming from a CRUMPLED piece of cloth lying in the corner of the room. Upon walking closer to it Kamakshi squealed, "Amma, there it is, my white and blue sock."

A Sock of surprise

As Amma and Kamakshi observed it closely, it seemed that strangely enough, her sock had now grown a head, a face and two little ears.

"Oh no," Kamakshi said and closed her mouth with her hands. Her sock had now come to life. Like magic. Or was it something else? The mornings were getting colder and it seemed that a **SQUIRREL** in search of some warmth, had borrowed Kamakshi's sock and made it his home.

Amma said, "We need to take the squirrel out of the sock. But the poor thing looks so scared."

"Don't do that, Amma," Kamakshi said, "It is alright to go to school with a single sock. And maybe if I take the squirrel along, my teacher won't scold me."

And so into a brown WOODEN basket the sock and the squirrel were placed and Kamakshi got into her school van wearing just one sock.

At the bus stop, the children crowded around her and peeped into her little basket. The squirrel still looked scared and refused to bring out his head.

At school, Kamakshi walked up to her teacher and explained the story behind her single sock. The teacher smiled☺ at Kamakshi and asked, "So, what is the name of your new friend?"

Thinking for a bit, Kamakshi answered, "His name is Socker, and don't you think that is just perfect?"

"Perfect," the teacher agreed and Kamakshi walked with her basket to leave Socker in the playground, while she went back to her class.

"Will you be alright alone till school gets over," Kamakshi asked in a sad voice. The SUN ☀ was out by then and Socker didn't seem cold or scared anymore and *Whoosh!* he popped out of her sock.

~ ☀ ~

11

MAZE

Kamakshi lost Sasha, her pet. Help her find him.

* Answer on the last page.

THE RIGHT DECISION

By R. K. VASHISTHA

It was the very first day after the summer vacation. For Neha, the summer vacation was a thrilling EXPERIENCE. Her face was beaming with happiness and she wanted to share it with all her friends.

She alone knew how hard it had been for her to convince her parents. She recalled the day when her parents were

discussing which hobby class would be the best for Neha during her **SUMMER** vacation.

Papa said, 'Neha is good at drawing. I think a drawing class is all that she needs right now.'

Mom said, 'But, she is equally good at computers. She knows the basics. I think she should join a **language** course. This will help her a lot. Moreover, there is a computer centre near our residence. And Mrs Sharma, the director is a good friend of mine. She will take absolute care of Neha.'

Neha's Demand

Her parents kept on **discussing** to arrive at the right decision but no one asked what she actually wanted to do. Finally, she said, 'I am not being asked what I should do.'

Her parents laughed.

Papa said, 'That's true. Tell us what you want to do?'

Neha said, 'Papa, I don't want to join any **HOBBY** classes.'

"What?" asked mom in disbelief.

"So, you want to just waste your time? Neha, this is the era of competition. You must prepare yourself for the **FUTURE**," Papa said.

Neha said, 'Papa, I want to go to Manali, the famous **hill station** in Himachal Pradesh. I have never been to any hill station. Please papa.'

There was pin-drop silence in the drawing-room. Both mom and papa kept on looking at each other for quite some time. The silence was unbearable for Neha. Finally, after an aeon mom said, 'It is very far from here and we have never been to north India. Moreover, it is going to be expensive. I don't think we can afford that.'

This was a bad news for Neha. She looked at papa with **watery** eyes. There was still some hope and she didn't want to give up that soon.

In a very serious tone papa began, 'Your mom is right. She alone handles the family **budget**. I don't think we can…'

15

Papa's idea

Neha had begun sobbing. Papa said, 'Let me finish, Neha. I don't think, we can say no to you. But you have to prove that my decision to say yes is the right decision. And for that you have to work.'

'Yes papa. I promise to work. I will help mom in all house hold work', Neha said with excitement.

Papa laughed, 'Not this kind of work, dear. What I want you to do is to carry a diary and a pen with you and reCord the names of various places and specialty of those places. I will help you wherever you need. This will be a right combination of fun and knowledge.'

Neha smiled and before mom could say something, papa had lifted her on his shoulders and was running from one room to another leaving mom in the drawing room. What a day it was!

Neha was still in her thoughts when she heard the bell. After the regular prayers, the principal began asking the students about what they all did during their summer vacation. Most of those who VOLUNTEERED to talk had done the usual hobby classes, while others had visited their relatives. Then came Neha's turn.

"I went to Manali", she said in a little louder voice so that everybody could hear her.

Everybody looked at her with **surprise**. The principal called her to the stage, "Neha, come here and tell all of us what all you saw in Manali."

Neha wanted to share her travelogue with her close friends and not with every one. But how could she defy the order of the principal? As she walked to the stage, every one cheered her. The principal adjusted the mike to suit her height.

Neha began, "I am thankful to my **PARENTS** for accepting my request to plan a visit to Manali. It is one of the most beautiful places in India and I had seen it in many films.

The beautiful journey

"MANALI is in Himachal Pradesh and is about 1920 km from Mumbai. We went to New Delhi by Rajdhani Express and thereafter by a Volvo bus to Manali. It is about 600 km from Delhi. It was 18-hours JOURNEY by bus. The bus stopped at many places like Panipat, Ambala, Chandigarh, Bilaspur and Mandi.

We got down at Kullu. At Kullu, we visited Manikaran which is famous for hot springs. You can tie raw RICE in cotton cloth bag and suspend it in hot water spring for half an hour. When you pull it up, the rice is already cooked and you can have it right away. And it is very tasty. Kullu is famous all over the world for shawls industry and DUSSEHRA festival.

"From there we took a cab to Manali. We stayed there for 3 days and visited all the famous places like Snow Point, Roerich Art Gallery, Naggar, Hidimba Temple, Vashisth Kund and Tibetan Monastery. We also saw Botanical Garden."

Neha looked at the principal, "Sir, I learnt a SECRET there."

"What's that, Neha?"", the principal asked as the whole gathering listened attentively.

"Sir, in most of the bollywood films what we are shown as Kashmir is basically Manali."

This information was new to most of the students and teachers. So they shouted "Wow!"

Suddenly the principal said, "Thank you, Neha." Then he turned to the students, and asked, "Does anybody want to visit Manali?"

There was a big "YES!"

"Okay. So, next year in summer vacation let's take a **SCHOOL** trip to Manali and see everything with our eyes. But there is one problem. Who is going to be our guide?"

The whole school shouted, "Neha".

Neha was pleasantly **surprised**. She recalled her papa's advice: Fun and knowledge can go hand in hand.

~ ☀ ~

WHO BUILT THE QUTUB MINAR

By Ilika Priye

Ravi was visiting his **COUSIN** in Delhi. His uncle and aunt were taking him to Mehrauli because he really wanted to see the Qutub Minar. Ravi had read in books that the Qutub Minar was the tallest brick tower in the world. He was excited about seeing it for real.

He knew that the Qutub Minar was built by Qutub-ud-Din-Aibak in the year 1199. But there was so much more that he wanted to know. They soon reached the spot. Ravi looked around **EAGERLY**.

"Oh! I didn't realise how tall this monument actually is!" said Ravi, in wonder.

"Yes, it is! It's about **73 metres tall**," said someone.

An informative friend

Ravi turned and saw a young boy clad in worn-out **TATTERED** clothes standing beside him.

Ravi ignored him because the boy's hands and legs were dusty. His hair was unkempt too. Ravi wanted to see the Qutub Minar. He walked ahead, and after reaching closer, he said, "The tower looks wide from below, but narrow from the top!"

"Yes, the base diameter is about 15 metres wide at the bottom, but it reduces to 2.5 metres diameter at the top. This tapering structure required architectural skill to build," said the boy again.

Ravi looked at him in **surprise**. He thought, "I'm not talking to him, and yet he keeps answering. And how does he know so much?"

Ravi decided to test him. He asked, "How many stories are there in the tower?"

"The Qutub Minar is 72.5 metres tall and it has five stories. The iron pillars in the premises that you will soon see have not caught rust despite being almost 900 years old," said the boy.

Ravi was surprised again. And he was impressed. He asked the boy, "You know a lot! What's your name?"

"My name is Sumit. I live nearby."

"My name's Ravi. I'm visiting my uncle and aunt here in **Delhi**," said Ravi shaking hands with Sumit.

They both were around the same age. Although Sumit was untidy and his clothes were tattered, Ravi became friendly with him.

All about the Qutub Minar

Sumit told him more about the Qutub Minar:

"Qutub-ud-Din-Aibak, the first ruler of the Delhi Sultanate, started the construction of the Qutub Minar but he built only the basement. Iltutmish, the successor of Qutub-ud-Din-Aibak, built the three stories after that. The top was damaged by LIGHTNING. Then Firoz Shah Tughlaq, the third ruler of the Tughlaq Dynasty, reconstructed it and built the last two stories."

"Why is the tower TILTED?" asked Ravi who was roaming with Sumit now.

"Because it has been repaired and reconstructed many times. The top stories were added a few years later," said Sumit.

"But tell me something."

"Yes?"

"How do you know so much about this **monument**?"

"My family is related to its history," said Sumit.

"How are they related?" asked Ravi, surprised.

"My ancestor was one of the labourers who was employed to build this monument. He worked under the instructions of Qutub-ud-Din-Aibak. When Iltutmish took over, my ancestor's successor was employed. After the top part was damaged by lightning in 1368, and when it was being reconstructed, another **ANCESTOR** of mine was a labourer. Whenever the Qutub Minar has been repaired or reconstructed, someone or the other from my family has been involved in it. I belong to a family of those labourers," said Sumit.

"So, that's why you know so much!" said Ravi.

"Yes," said Sumit, in a sad voice. He then became thoughtful.

A new insight

"What's wrong?" asked Ravi.

"You see, it's the construction **WORKERS** and the labourers who are most involved in the building of any historical monument. But no one remembers them. Qutub-ud-Din-Aibak constructed the Qutub Minar, but my ancestors put in the hard work and labour. But no one asks about them," said Sumit, dejectedly.

Ravi was taken aback. He had never thought about this. Sumit was right. Not just Qutub Minar, there are so many historical monuments and nobody knows about the people who worked to build them, how much they toiled and how they **LIVED**.

Ravi thought for a while and said, "You're right, my friend! We should at least know how many people were involved and how much effort they put in. Do you stay nearby?"

"Yes, I stay nearby. My father is a labourer too. He does the cleaning of construction sites, and so do I. We often visit this monument and look after it. We love it a lot. So much of our ancestors' work went into its construction," smiled Sumit.

Ravi looked at the Qutub Minar thoughtfully, and said, "I can't even imagine the EFFORT that went into the construction of this monument!"

They roamed around for a bit. Then Ravi went home with his uncle and aunt. He had learned a lot about the historical monument today.

He decided to go back home and tell everyone about Sumit and how his ancestors worked hard to build the Qutub Minar and decided to also know about the lives of LABOURERS who built other monuments.

MAP QUEST

Going on a trip is always fun. Read the hints below and find out which three places Zeba went to.

* Zeba went to a historical country where pharaohs lived.

* She went further down in the African continent and saw Mount Kilimanjaro.

* She visited an island that shares the same name as an animated movie.

* Answers on the last page.

THE 'FORWARD' SCAM

By Omprakash Kshatriya

Devaansh picked up his mobile and opened a message. It read:

'Dear Devaansh! May you always remain happy in life!

Son, I read the message that you sent me. It was a **forwarded** message that said, 'If you want to pass your exams, then send this message to 40 people or you will get bad luck and 'will fail'.

Believing in the truth

I wish to share something with you and hope that you will always remember it. When I was in class 8, I had received a similar **LETTER** in our school. Everyone in my class got one. I found one in my bag and after reading it, I was really anxious and scared. I looked around in shock and did not know what to do. Luckily, our teacher walked into the classroom at the very moment.

He was a highly learned man who was practical. He knew something was wrong when he saw me standing frozen with **FEAR**. He asked me, "What is it, Gautami? Why do you look so frightened?"

I handed the letter to him immediately. He started to laugh when he read the letter and said, "Don't let this bother you. I have a **SOLUTION** to your problem. Let me give you another letter that can counter the effects of the letter that you have received."

"Is that true, Guruji? Is it really possible?" I asked.

"Of course, it is possible. But, for it to come true, you have to obey certain rules," he said sternly.

The letter had made me extremely **NERVOUS** as I had to prepare for a math **exam** the next day. How could I make 40 handwritten copies of the letter and distribute them to all the students in my class? That would take an entire day and leave me with no time to prepare for the exam. The contents of the letter and the instructions made me anxious.

According to the letter, I would get bad **luck** if I did not follow the instructions written on it. I pleaded "I am willing to follow every rule, but please save me from this problem and the misfortune it may cause."

A scary trail

Guruji called another teacher from our school and asked her to write a letter for me. He gave me the letter and said, "The first rule is to keep this letter in an **ISOLATED** corner along with your books and make sure that you do not open and read it before your results are announced. Otherwise, it will not be able to **protect** you from bad luck."

"I will do as you say," I agreed instantly. The earlier letter also had a warning against throwing it away. It even mentioned names of people who had not BELIEVED in the letter like Ramlal, who ignored the letter and his son had died a week later; Ghanshyam, who tore the letter, and suffered huge losses in his business; Kishore who failed in his exams as he had not followed the instructions of the letter.

The letter mentioned many scary events and since I did not understand such things, it made me feel more scared. But after Guruji gave me the other letter that could counter the effects of this letter, I felt empowered.

"Nothing can stop you from excelling in your exams," Guruji promised, "All you have to do is to work hard so you can write your exam well."

His words brought back the confidence I had lost and I studied very hard for my exams. I solved all the problems in my maths exam the next day. When the results were announced, I had excelled and as promised I carried both the letters to school.

Where's the magic?

Guruji CONGRATULATED me on my result and said, "Did I not tell you that you will excel your exam?"

I was very happy and said, "You made it possible by giving me this magical letter. It was the magic in the letter that helped me pass my exams."

Guruji laughed at my comment and said, "Gautami! There is no magic in that letter. When we doubt ourselves, we are not able to perform and get **POOR** results."

Guruji's words didn't make any sense to me. "I am unable to understand. Please explain," I pleaded.

Guruji then asked me to take out the letter he'd given me and read it again.

When I opened the letter I was surprised to see it written in **Urdu**. I did not know how to read Urdu and said, "But I can't read this letter."

"Give the letter to Zareena. Let her read it out for you," he said.

As Zareena started to read the letter, I felt like the earth under my feet was shaking.

Zareena read, "You have to **WRITE** this letter 40 times in your own handwriting and give it to 40 children in your classroom. If you fail to do so then you will not be able to clear your exams. Your Teacher, Narendra."

"Please read it once again, Zareena. Are you sure it says that I will not clear my exam if I do not make 40 copies of this letter and DISTRIBUTE them?" I repeated.

"Yes Gautami, that is what the letter says but you still cleared your exam because you studied hard for your exam. Since you wrote your exam with confidence, you were able to excel in them. The letter had nothing to do with it," explained Guruji.

"I had the letter written in Urdu so that even if you opened the letter out of curiosity, you would not understand what was written in it. This was the best way to REMOVE the fear of the earlier letter from your mind," he added.

The simple mind trick

"Guruji, you are right. If I had read this letter, I would have lost confidence and would not have been able to concentrate on my studies. I wouldn't have worked as hard and wouldn't have excelled in my exams. You gave me CONFIDENCE and I am grateful to you."

"Well done! Never fall for such superstitions in future," he said and patted my back.

My teacher was none other than Narendra Dabholkar who was born on November 1, 1945, in the Satara District of Maharashtra. He was shot because he was a rationalist and became a martyr in 2013.

I, therefore, request you to refrain from writing and forwarding **MESSAGES** and letters that spread fear and SUPERSTITION.

Such messages are sent to make you weak. Believe in yourself and know that you can score marks with hard work and confidence.

In this era of mobile phones, I am sending this letter as a picture so that you can save it with you forever. I have full confidence and in you that if you work hard, you will definitely clear your exams.

Your Loving Mother.

~ 🌟 ~

THE DRAGON AND THE RABBIT

By Rimmy Lahri

A long time ago in Peace Forest, there lived Dino the Dragon with master Golu, a green giant. Golu took good care of Dino. He would go **hunting** every day and return with a rabbit for him. Dino was very happy living with his master.

A little girl Aashi and her pet rabbit Rojo lived next to Golu's house. One day, Golu fell ILL and could not go to the forest to hunt for Dino's food.

Hungry Dino did not know what to do. He thought of venturing to the FOREST to find food but his master gave him an idea.

Golu said, "Why do you have to go so far when you can eat the rabbit next door?"

A hungry intent

Dino liked Golu's suggestion and went to Aashi's house.

Unaware of Dino's intentions, Aashi and Rojo invited Dino inside their home. Dino saw Rojo lay cosy in Aashi's ARMS as she brushed his soft fur. He realised that it would be difficult to eat Rojo as he was Aashi's pet.

Aashi offered a chair to Dino but as soon as he sat, it broke into pieces. Aashi suggested that they all sit on the FLOOR.

After some time, Dino couldn't stay hungry and asked Aashi if she had something to eat.

Keeping his size in mind, Aashi served him lots of grass, cabbage leaves, carrots, chickpeas and a little cottage cheese on a big plate. She served him some milk and water too.

Dino had never eaten such food but because Aashi forced him, he took a small bite but didn't enjoy the TASTE at all. He thought of sipping some milk but spat it out. He craved to eat a rabbit.

Hungry and angry, he growled, "I am **HUNGRY**, I want to eat this rabbit."

Frightened, Aashi grabbed Rojo and said, "You cannot **EAT** him. He is my pet just like you are Golu's pet. How can I let him be your food?"

Dino sat silently. He understood that Aashi **loved** Rojo just like his master loved and cared for him.

A new dish

Aashi added, "Rojo eats this food that is why I offered it to you. If you don't like it **RaW**, I can cook it for you. It will taste better."

"How do you cook food?" asked Dino. "Food is cooked on fire," replied Aashi.

Dino found it interesting that Aashi used fire, just like him. He said, "I can create fire! I breathe fire. If you want, I can **COOK** this food right now."

"Then what are you waiting for?" invited Aashi.

A big ball of fire came out of Dino's mouth and cooked the food in the bowl.

Aashi quickly added some salt and **pepper**  to the roasted food and asked Dino to try it.

Dino took a small bite and to his surprise, he found it delicious. He finished everything that was in the bowl and thanked Aashi for it. He promised never to eat rabbits and made friends with Rojo.

From that day, the three of them played together. Aashi always had a **SNACK** ready for Dino and Golu was happy that now he didn't have to hunt every day.

THE BRAVE BROTHERS

Aparna Majumbdar

Satpuravan was very dense and beautiful. There was greenery everywhere. The forest had many big, **TALL** and expansive trees.

For a few days, the trees were being slyly **cut**. Despite heavy security, it was not found out when the thieves came, felled the trees and went away.

In order to stop the cutting of the trees in the forest, Forest Inspector Pratap Singh began to keep guard **NIGHT** and **day**, but the forest was so big and dense that when one corner was guarded, the thieves would cut trees from the other corner and go away.

In the middle of the forest there was a small village of tribals, Ranipur, where about eight to ten families lived. There was no school therefore the children would play the whole day in the forest and go home in the **EVENING**.

Sahil and Suraj were two brothers who lived in the village. Their parents worked during the day in the villages nearby and came home in the evening.

Sahil and Suraj would also play in the forest the whole day and were familiar with every **NOOK** and corner. They loved the forest as if it was their friend.

They would get angry whenever they saw the felled trees. Both brothers would roam about from one corner to the other to search the thieves. Wandering in the forest they met Forest Inspector Pratap Singh.

"Forest Uncle did you come to know about the thieves?" Sahil and Suraj asked together.

Catching the thieves

"No children! There is no news as yet, but we will catch them soon. If you have any information let me know immediately.

Sahil suddenly woke up one night. He was sleeping in the hut. There was a window in the hut. He saw a light from the **window**. He got up and went to the window and looked out.

Since it was a moonless night, he could see the light clearly. His brain began working fast. He tried to wake his parents up but they were sound asleep and could not hear Sahil's voice.

Sahil woke up his **YOUNGER** brother Suraj, "Get up Suraj, thieves have come to the forest".

"Where?" said Suraj getting up.

"Probably near the pond, get up quickly we have to catch the thieves".

Suraj stood up

Sahil dragged him out of the house. "Come let us go and see what they are doing".

Both brothers moved towards the light in the dark **NIGHT**. When they went near, they saw a truck parked. Some criminal type of men with modern tools in their hands were cutting trees. They were bringing down the trees with the help of ropes, therefore there was no sound.

Sahil whispered, "Go inform Uncle Forest, till then I will

stop these thieves."

"Alright Brother, look after yourself".

"Yes, you too… Bring Uncle Forest soon, because they have modern tools, with which they are cutting the trees quickly. Now I understand why no one came to know about their cutting the trees".

The Timely Act

Suraj went to call the **police** .

Sahil hid in the bushes nearby to keep an eye on the thieves.

The thieves felled many **TREES** within no time.

Sahil reached the truck slowly, avoiding the eyes of the

thieves.

"Do it quickly", someone commanded in a whisper but in a strong voice.

"Boss one tree is left. We will keep it and go".

The work of the thief finished but Suraj did not come with the police. 'Is Suraj safe? I have sent him alone in the dark. Some wild animals may…no no nothing has happened to my brother'. Sahil **shivered** as he thought about Suraj.

He wanted to stop the thieves, but how? The tyre of the truck was so thick that it could not be punctured.

Sahil looked around. Many big stones were lying near him. He picked up the stones and placed them in front of the tyre, in order to stop the truck for a while.

The driver started the truck, but it did not move from its position.

"Go down and see what has happened?" Boss said.

Two-three thieves got down from the truck and looked under the truck. Then they saw Sahil.

"Boss a boy is hiding under the **TRUCK**".

"Catch him and bring him".

Sahil understood from the boss's words that they would kill him if he was caught.

As soon as the thieves bent down, Sahil threw a fistful of 𝕤𝕒𝕟𝕕 in their faces.

It went in their eyes. They started screaming rubbing their eyes.

A brave step

Getting a chance Sahil ran in the same DIRECTION as his younger brother had taken. He was more worried about his younger brother than himself. He wanted to quickly search for his brother.

Boss told the other persons in the truck, "Go, catch the boy and bring him. Otherwise you had it".

At that moment Forest Inspector Pratap Singh's voice was heard. "All of you are surrounded. You will be shot if you try to run".

With this announcement all around, search lights were switched on. The eyes of the thieves were **dazzled** by the strong light.

Sahil saw his younger brother standing near Forest Uncle. He went and hugged his brother.

Next day the photos of the two **BROTHERS** were in the newspapers. The government gave them rewards and arranged for their education in school.

FUN WITH POETRY

By Omprakash Kshatriya

As soon as the new teacher, Mr Ramesh, entered the **CLASSROOM**, the students said, "Sir! Today is Laughter Day in school. We don't want to study."

"You pulled the words right out of my mouth," said Mr Ramesh putting the book down on the table. "Even I don't want to teach today."

Poetry Time

The students clapped together and said, "Wow! What fun! No lessons today!"

"Come, let's play a game!" he said. "We'll make silly poems to express ourselves today!"

"Sir, we do want to play, but didn't understand what are we supposed to do," said Yogesh. "Can you explain what the game exactly is?"

"Today, we will speak in rhymes!" said Mr Ramesh.

"Whatever we say, we have to make it rhyme like a **POEM**. So if we want to say something, I will say it in two lines. For example:

My Grandpa—I tell,

Chews his food well!
Or you could say:

Akash, go play on the ground,
Don't just laze around!"

Devansh was excited about this. He had a flair for writing poetry. He stood up at once and said:

"It's raining without a cloud.
Sir, may I go out?"

And he raised his little **FINGER**  to show the teacher that he wanted to be excused to use the bathroom.

The other students started laughing.

Mr Ramesh guffawed. He said:

"Rush out the door,
Don't spill on the floor!
But do come back;
            I'm not a bore!"

And he signalled Devansh that he was excused.

Meanwhile, Rahul was suffering from an **upset** stomach. He had to go to the bathroom too.

But he could not think of a poem to ask for permission.

He told his friend, Vikas, "Man! I have to go to the bathroom!"

"Here, take this," said Vikas handing over a NOTEBOOK to him. It had some lines written on it. "Say this, and you will get permission to use the bathroom."

Rahul took the book, stood up, and said:

"The time is tough,
The situation, rough!
If I don't go now,
I'll just huff and puff!"

Rahul pointed at his tummy, gesturing that he needed to go to the **BATHROOM** urgently.

Mr Ramesh understood his problem and said:

"On your feet, off you go,
Come back fast; I'm not saying 'no'!"

All the children were enjoying today's **class** a lot. Nikunj who was sitting ahead felt that instead of speaking in **rhymes**, they should go to the playground and play some sport. He said, "Sir!"

"Yes, yes, tell me!

Ideas and thoughts, any?"

Nikunj said:

"Sitting and talking,
Speaking and rhyming,
Enough of that—
Any time for playing?"

He pointed outside, trying to say that they **enjoyed** the rhyming game and should now be allowed to go outside and play.

But the other students were still enjoying the rhymes.

They shook their hands and said, "No, we don't want to go outside!"

Mr Ramesh said:

"My friend! Laugh out loud,
Make them proud,
But do as you please,
Learn with ease!"

"Yes, Sir!" said the other students and started laughing.

The period was soon over. The **bell** rang and Mr Ramesh prepared to leave.

The students said, "Sir, please stay back a little while. We're enjoying this class so much!"

"Children! This is just the **beginning**! Just wait and see how much more fun we'll have! Remember that it is important to have fun while studying and playing. Keep doing that, and we'll all move forward with gusto," he said and left.

The students had fun celebrating Laughter Day. Their day was spent and rhyming

~ ✷ ~

SEQUENCE

It was the first day of e-school for Nisha.
Arrange the scenes in order to know how her day went.

* Answer on the last page.

FRIENDSHIP

By Madhu Goel

A small group of children had started organising a **RACING** competition on weekends in the nearby park. They even collected money and gave out prizes to the winners to maintain the spirit of competition and enthusiasm.

Rohan watched the children enjoying and participating in the races from a bench every weekend. He always left after the races feeling sad.

Sohan had been observing Rohan since the first week. This time, he went up to Rohan and asked, "Why do you sit here quietly? You can also enjoy participating in the races. You will have **fun**."

"No, no! You all please carry on," Rohan replied.

"Why? Don't you like to run?" asked Sohan.

"No, it is not that." Rohan replied, but his voice choked.

"What happened? Did I say something wrong?" Sohan asked.

"No, that's not it!" replied Rohan.

"Then why did you stop mid-sentence, my friend?" asked Sohan. Rohan took a deep breath and replied, "Actually, I lost one of my LEGS in an accident."

"Oh! I am very sorry to hear that, but from now on we are friends. Come, let me introduce you to my other friends. What is your name?" Sohan asked.

"Rohan!"

"I am Sohan, and look, our names are so similar—Rohan and Sohan," Sohan said excitedly.

Finding Friends

"Difficulties are a part of life, and they come and go, but you should never lose HEART. These days you can get an artificial leg and lead a normal life, so don't give too much importance to your handicap. Keep a POSITIVE attitude and fulfil all your dreams," Sohan motivated Rohan.

"I am sure you must have heard of Arunima Singh. She climbed Mount Everest despite being disabled," Sohan continued.

"Yes, I know about ARTIFICIAL legs; my father has applied for one," Rohan answered.

"Anyway, this weekend, we will hold a one-legged race, and you can also participate in it," Sohan suggested.

"But why do you want to SPOIL the fun for everybody for my sake; I will be happy watching all of you," Rohan hesitated.

"Don't worry about that. Come, let me introduce you to my friends," Sohan replied.

After the introduction, the children collected the money for the PRIZE and Rohan also contributed towards it.

Rohan was very HAPPY when he reached home. He told his parents about what had happened.

"That is great! So, how many friends did you make today?" his mother asked.

"There were ten children in all, and one of them was Sohan. Ma, I do not feel lonely anymore," he said.

"Yes, my son, that is how friendship makes you feel," Ma agreed.

Race at the park

Next week Rohan reached the park at the designated **time**. Everyone was happy to see him. Sumit was the judge for this weekend; the children took turns to be the judge every week.

The race started at the scheduled time, and everybody was surprised that Rohan won the race. They all clapped for him and **HUGGED** him. He was presented with a gift.

Rohan opened the gift in front of all his friends. He was happy to see a motivational book as his gift.

He had tears in his eyes about finding such wonderful friends and said, "Friendship, love, companionship, and understanding the pain of others are signs of a good **FRIENDSHIP**. I have learned all this from you."

"Rohan, don't you think that praise is more than what we deserve?" Sohan asked, and everybody laughed.

"Don't forget to come next weekend," Sohan reminded him.

"I can never forget you all. You all have supported me so much, and by the way, it is my birthday next Saturday," Rohan announced.

"Are you not going to call us for your birthday?" they asked in a chorus.

"Of course, I will! I want you to meet my parents," he answered.

"So what is the problem? We can have the **RACE** in the morning and celebrate your birthday in the evening," Sumit said.

"Alright, but I have a suggestion," Rohan said.

"What is it?" asked Sohan.

"I want you all to race, and I will observe you. I will be happy to see all my FRIENDS running," said Rohan.

"Agreed! But please don't stress yourself. And we would like it if you agreed to be the judge next weekend," said Sohan.

"Yes, I would love that," Rohan replied happily, and they all agreed.

Rohan saw the time on his wristwatch and said, "I should get back home; my mother must be worried."

"Okay, Rohan, see you on Saturday, but you don't have to be so formal with us. We are all friends, so just relax," Sohan said.

"Okay, friends," Rohan replied as he left.

"What held you up today?" asked Ma.

"We had a race today, and I won the **first** prize, Ma," said Rohan as he showed his gift to her.

Ma kissed him on his forehead.

"Can friends be so lovely, Ma?" he asked.

"Yes, my dear. There is no single definition of friendship, and you can call it by any name. True friendship does not involve **SELFISHNESS**. It creates a sense of belonging," Ma explained.

"Friends may not be able to remove our **PAIN** and sadness, but their presence helps us to feel less pain," she added.

"Yes, I have felt that too. When I am with my friends, I feel like I belong and that I am one of them. They do not make me feel like I am any different and that I am handicapped," Rohan said with tears in his eyes.

His mother kissed him again and said, "Never call yourself handicapped."

Next weekend, after the race, the children went to Rohan's house to celebrate his birthday.

Birthday fun

Rohan's father shared the good news that their application had been accepted for the artificial leg. They had been waiting for months. All the friends were happy.

"Now my Rohan can walk along with all his friends," said Rohan's mother.

They all SANG and danced and celebrated Rohan's birthday.

"Birthdays come every year, but my birthday this year has been EXTRA special. Firstly, because of the good news that Dad gave us and secondly because I have such good friends who helped me forget all my pain," said Rohan with gratitude.

GREENIE GOES FREE

By Satish Roy

It was Sonu's birthday and his dad had brought him a little parrot in a cage. Sonu loved it.

"Thank you dad!" he said giving him a hug. "Look at his **FEATHERS**," he said pointing to the parrot. "They're so green. I'll call him Greenie."

Sonu hung Greenie's cage in the balcony. He filled **WATER** in a bowl and placed it inside Greenie's cage with some fresh fruits.

"Will you be my friend, Greenie?" asked Sonu.

"*Kree-kree*," said Greenie and sulked in the corner of the cage.

The next morning, Sonu came to the balcony to check on Greenie.

"Good morning, Greenie," said Sonu with a smile.

A blue Greenie

Greenie just sat in the corner and sulked.

"You haven't eaten a thing," said Sonu, looking at the food in Greenie's **cage**. "Are you alright Greenie?" he asked peering inside.

"Looks like you're missing your family," said Sonu, feeling sad.

A few days passed and Greenie was still feeling blue.
Sonu tried hard to lift Greenie's spirits but nothing seemed to work.

One evening when Sonu came back from school, he saw Greenie looking up at the **sky** and flapping her wings. She was looking at all the **PARROTS** that lived in the trees nearby.

Sonu didn't understand what was going on.

Sonu went to bed that night, but for some reason, he couldn't sleep. The image of Greenie flapping her wings and feeling sad was ingrained in his mind. He tossed and turned for what seemed like a long time, until he heard a noise from the **BALCONY**.

The Invaders

Sonu decided to investigate. As he approached the balcony, he noticed two figures standing in the dark. They looked like humans, but something about them made them look different.

"Who are you? What do you want?" asked Sonu.

"We have come from **JUPITER**. We are here to take you with us," said one of the two figures.

"Jupiter? You are aliens!" said Sonu. "Why have you come for me?"

"Just like how you humans keep animals and **BIRDS** in cages, we are putting together a collection of creatures from different planets. You will be given a place to stay, food to eat and water to drink. No comfort will be spared, but you will not have the freedom to go where you please," said the other alien.

"No! I will not come with you," shouted Sonu and tried running away. But Sonu found that no matter how hard he

tried, he couldn't move.

The aliens carried him outside to their SPACESHIP. They took him inside and put him in a cage. The cage had everything Sonu had in his room. There was a bookshelf with lots of books, a comfortable bed and a study table. On the table was a plate full of snacks and a tall glass of juice.

Far from home

Sonu sat in the corner and SULKED as the aliens fiddled with their spaceship. After a while, one of the aliens came to Sonu and said, "It will take us a while to reach Jupiter. I suggest that you grab a bite to eat and make yourself comfortable."

"No!" said Sonu. "I don't want to go to Jupiter. I want to go home!"

"I'm afraid that can't happen, Sonu," said the alien. "You'll be staying with us for the rest of your life."

"No, no! Please let me go!" shouted Sonu.

"What's the matter Sonu? Are you having a bad dream?" asked the alien. It sounded just like his mom.

Sonu opened his eyes and saw that he was still in his room. His mom was by his bed, stroking his forehead. The sun was up and it was time to wake up.

"It was all a dream," said Sonu.

Free, at last!

"*Kree- kree,*" Sonu heard Greenie's voice from the balcony. He jumped out of bed and ran to her.

He carefully took the cage off its hook and took her to the garden. He opened the door to the cage and let her out. Greenie swooped out and sat on the **BRANCH** of a nearby tree.

Sonu found a cardboard box and tied it to the tree's branch.

"This will be your new home, Greenie," said Sonu.

"**Kree-kree,**" said Greenie, saying thanks this time.

~ ☀ ~

LAUGHING GHOSTS

By Inderjeet Kaushik

"This is not fair, Ma! It is just 9 AM and you have woken me up so **EARLY**," complained Sumaya as she walked towards the washbasin with her toothbrush in hand.

"And what makes you think that 9 AM is too early? Do you know we are up since 5 AM?" asked Ma. Sumaya made a face and started to brush her teeth disinterestedly.

Twelve-year-old Sumaya was extremely **LAZY** about getting up in the morning. She usually slept late and woke up late too. She lazed around in bed, lost in her thoughts even after waking up.

Her parents constantly advised her against **WASTING** time, "Darling, holidays should not be wasted like this. You should use this time to learn a new hobby or read books." But Sumaya ignored their advice and continued her habits.

Seeing no improvement in Sumaya's behaviour, Ma spoke to her brother, Anuj who said, "Why don't you send Sumaya to my place, Didi? Leave the rest to me."

Sumaya jumped with **JOY** as she was going to Uncle Anuj's house for a few days.

"Uncle Anuj loves me a lot and he won't nag me like Ma and Pa. This is going to be so much fun," she thought.

The exciting trip

Ma packed her bag and gave her necessary instructions before she **BOARDED** the bus to Uncle Anuj's village. "Do not trouble your uncle and listen to him."

"Sure, Ma," said Sumaya, **HUGGING** her mother before boarding the bus. She reached Uncle Anuj's village in two hours.

Safina, her cousin and Uncle Anuj's daughter, was waiting for her.

"I hope your journey was **comfortable**," asked Safina as she took Sumaya's bag. Sumaya nodded.

Soon, they reached home and she ran and hugged Uncle Anuj as soon as she saw him.

Uncle Anuj told Sumaya that she and Safina will be staying in their other house that was vacant. "Safina will help you if you need anything or if there is a problem," he said.

Safina took Sumaya with her to the other house. Uncle had made arrangements for them in different rooms. Sumaya liked the house and they spent the day talking and playing **CHESS** and went out in the evening.

At night, they went to their respective rooms to sleep.

Sleep Troubles

Sumaya could not sleep as the place was new, and also because she was not used to sleeping so early. Since she knew Ma was not there to wake her up early the next MORNING, she picked up a comic and started reading it and did not realise when she went to sleep.

She suddenly woke up and heard loud **laughter**. It was completely dark in the room and outside. Sumaya was sweating with fear. "This house seems to be haunted," she thought to herself. She tried to call Safina, but no sound came out of her mouth. She was scared to go to Safina's room.

In the morning, when Safina went to Sumaya's room, she found her **SITTING** on a chair, shivering with **fear**. Safina was surprised to see Sumaya like that and asked, "What happened, Sumaya? Why do you look so scared?"

"Please get me out of here. This place is haunted," said Sumaya and picked up her bag and held on to Safina. Safina calmed her down and asked her to tell what had happened that made her feel so scared.

After she heard Sumaya's story, Safina said, "There is no such thing as ghosts. You probably had a NIGHTMARE. Take a shower and get ready. My mother is waiting for us for breakfast," Safina consoled her.

Ghosts in the night!

The next night, the same thing happened. Sumaya was now sure that there were ghosts in the house and decided that she would not listen to anybody and take the afternoon bus back home.

Next morning, when Safina came to her room, Sumaya said, "I am not staying here at any cost. I want to go back."

Safina could not control her laughter. "Don't be scared. Tonight, I will **SLEEP** with you in this room and find out who is troubling you with this laughter," said Safina. This convinced Sumaya and she agreed to stay for another night.

That night the same thing happened and Sumaya woke up. She shook Safina and said, "Get up, Safina! I hear the laughter. Can you hear it too?" Safina sat up and for a moment she too was scared when she heard the laughter.

She soon regained her composure and asked Sumaya to stay back and went out to see who was laughing. The **SOUND** was coming from outside. Safina followed the direction of the laughter.

She had walked a little distance and at a park behind the house, she saw 10 to 12 people laughing together.

"Come, you are **Welcome** to join our laughter club. You can laugh with us as it helps to release all stress," invited a member.

The laughter club

Safina understood what was going on and she went back to Sumaya and said, "Come, let me take you to meet the laughing ghosts."

Safina took Sumaya to the park and pointed at the **people** and said, "Meet the laughing ghosts who laugh to release their tension. They have created a laughter club in this park."

Sumaya realised, that these people woke up early and came to laugh **together** Because she slept late, their early morning laughter seemed like an eerie ghost laugh to her.

It was Sumaya's turn to laugh now. She tried to control her laughter and said, "Why don't we join their laughter club?"

Safina joined her and they both laughed heartily. Sumaya was not scared of ghosts anymore.

After this incident, Sumaya changed her routine. She started to wake up early and go for walks in the park. A few days of walking in the fresh air and practising **yoga** made Sumaya realise the importance of getting up early and taking care of her health.

Uncle Anuj was EXTREMELY happy to see this change in Sumaya, and he could not wait to share with his sister how Sumaya had changed after coming to the village.

~ ✸ ~

Parts of this image have been left blank.
Look at the picture, complete it and then colour it.

TRISHA'S TIMELY LESSON

By Seema Nirupam

As soon as Trisha returned from school, she kicked off her shoes, FLUNG her bag in a corner and plonked herself on the sofa.

She switched on the television and called out to her mother, "Mom! I'm hungry!"

"First, change your CLOTHES and then you can eat your lunch," said her mother.

"I'll change after lunch. I won't spill anything on my uniform," replied Trisha.

"You still have to wash up," said her mother.

No value for time

Trisha ignored her mother and continued watching the TELEVISION. After a few minutes, her friend Tina called up on the landline and they began to chat.

73

"Trisha, your lunch is ready. Come and have your food," her mother called.

"Mom, I am discussing something important with Tina. I'll come in a few minutes," replied Trisha and continued to chat with her friend.

Just when she was done with her call, the **DOORBELL** rang. Trisha opened the door to find their neighbour, Aunt Nitu standing outside.

"Hello, Aunt Nitu! Come on in," said Trisha.

"Why are you still in your school **UNIFORM**?" asked Aunt Nitu, walking in.

"Umm...well, I was going to change," replied Trisha, smiling sheepishly.

"Anyway, I have been trying to call you for the past 20 minutes but your phone was busy. You said you wanted to see that magic show, right? Guess what! I got two **TICKETS** for it," said Aunt Nitu.

"Wow! Thank you!" said Trisha happily.

"Now hurry up and get ready. We have to reach there by 4. So, we have to leave home in 15 minutes. If we are late, we won't be allowed inside," said Aunt Nitu.

The rush

Trisha rushed to her room to CHANGE.

"Oh, dear! Now, where will I find my clothes in this mess?" she wondered looking at her room. "I should have cleaned my room yesterday when Mom asked me to."

Trisha quickly changed into the first clean dress she found. She did not have the time to freshen up or comb her hair. When she rushed back to the living room, she saw her lunch on the table. Her tummy growled in HUNGER but there was no time to eat.

"If only I had eaten LUNCH as soon as I came back from school…" she regretted.

"Mom, where are my black **SANDALS**?" Trisha asked, frantically searching the **SHOE** cabinet.

"I don't know. Where did you leave them last evening after coming back home from the park?" asked her mother.

Trisha looked everywhere and finally found them under the sofa.

"Aunt Nitu won't take me **anywhere** after today. Not only am I late, I am not even dressed properly," thought Trisha.

"Shall we get going, Trisha?" asked Aunt Nitu. "I have to fill fuel as well."

The delay

While on their way in the **CAR**, Trisha was almost in tears. It was going to be 4. If they are not allowed inside, it would be her fault.

"I am so sorry, Aunt Nitu. I don't think we will reach on time. I am *SORRY* that the tickets are going to go to waste because of me," said Trisha.

"It's okay, Trisha. The magic show is actually at 6," said Aunt Nitu, smiling at her. "Your mother and I planned this so that you understand the value of **TIME**. Your mother has been worried about you. She told me that you often come back late from the park and don't have time to finish your **HOMEWORK** in the evening. You end up doing it in the morning, and thus skip breakfast. You also keep postponing things instead of doing them right away."

"Yes, Aunt Nitu. I realise the importance of doing things on time. I'll try to be punctual," said Trisha.

"Now, come on. Let's eat something before we head for the show. I know you are hungry," said Aunt Nitu.

"Oh yes! Thank you, Aunt Nitu," said a **GRATEFUL** Trisha.

~ ~

CROSSING THE BARRIERS

By S. Varalakshmi

On a WARM day in Chennai, Swetha ran into the kitchen and yelled, "Amma, do you know what I learnt today?"

Her mother, Prema asked with a smile, "What?"

"*Ich liebe dich*, Amma," Swetha tilted her head and said with a smile.

"What does that mean?" Prema asked.

"It means 'I love you, Amma' in German," Swetha said proudly.

"Wonderful, Swetha. I see you are already forming sentences," said her mother.

Then she enthusiastically screamed, "*Ich liebe all.*"

"Don't you know the German word for 'all'?" her elder brother Ganesh teased.

Swetha cleared her throat pretending not to have heard the remark.

Her father stroked her hair and said, "Talk about co-incidences! Just yesterday, a German FAMILY moved in next door. They have a daughter who is your age. I am sure she will love to talk to someone who knows German."

An exchange of languages

Swetha's eyes lit up at the thought of having a new friend.

She then caught sight of Ganesh eating something from a bowl.

Eyeing it hungrily, she asked, "What are you eating, *bruder* (brother in German)?"

Knowing that Swetha was showing off her beginner's flair for the language, he shot back, "*Verse Patat.*"

"What is that?" she asked.

"French fries in Dutch. Bet you didn't know that!" he replied with a smile.

Swetha **SMILED** sheepishly and without warning, lunged and grabbed some French fries from his bowl. And saying a hurried goodbye, left the house.

She ran into a blue-eyed girl standing outside, looking a bit lost.

With no hesitation, Swetha greeted, "**GUTEN TAG**."

The girl looked at her in surprise and then with a friendly smile she too said, "*Guten Tag. Sprechen Sie Deustch?* (Do you speak German?)"

Swetha nodded and said, "*Ja* (yes). Sprechen Sie English?"

The girl replied, "Ohh yes, I am Heidi. What's your name?"

"Swetha. I live next door. I'm glad to meet you. How do you like it here so far?"

"I was feeling a bit lost before but after meeting you, I feel fine. What's your mother tongue?" Heidi asked.

"Tamil. It is one of the oldest **LANGUAGES** of India," said Swetha.

"Oh wow! I would love to know about your cultural heritage. Would you please teach me Tamil? Since I am new to Chennai and don't understand Tamil, I find it hard to interact with others."

Swetha laughed and said, "**KANNDIPA** meaning 'definitely' in Tamil, Heidi. That would be my pleasure. There, you have learnt your first word in Tamil already. And will you please teach me German?" Heidi nodded and both looked forward to learning new languages.

New Friends

Swetha took Heidi hOmE to meet her family.

Heidi was an easygoing girl and got along with them very well.

Prema brought her a plate of Masala Dosa and a glass of *Ellaneer* (tender coconut water) which Heidi loved very much.

Then the children decided to go out to look around.

Before leaving the house, Swetha's parents asked Heidi to come visit them again, to which Heidi replied in Tamil, "*Kanndipa.*"

They all had a good laugh and soon the children left.

On the way, they met Swetha's principal Damodar who asked, "*Epdi Irruke* (How are you), Swetha?"

"*Na Nanna irruken* (I am fine), Sir," Swetha said with a smile.

Swetha then introduced Heidi to Damodar who in turn offered his hand to Heidi and asked, "How do you do, Heidi?"

Smilingly with a little **HESITATION** and an accent, Heidi replied, "*Na Nanna irruken*, sir."

Astonished, Damodar and Swetha looked at her. Heidi had picked the conversation between Damodar and Swetha.

"Fantastic, Heidi," Swetha exclaimed.

"Excellent, Heidi. By the way, have you decided which school to go to?"

"No, sir. But I would be happy if I could join your school, with your approval and permission, of course," replied Heidi.

"We would be happy to have you, Heidi," Damodar said.

"Sir, please visit my house anytime you are **FREE**. My parents would love to meet you and you Swetha," she replied.

They decided to go to Heidi's house to visit her parents.

Heidi's parents, Walter and Mia were sitting with Swetha's parents and brother, who had come to say hello to the new **NEIGHBOURS**. Swetha's mother handed a bag of fruits to Mia, as they were visiting them for the first time, for which Mia thanked her.

Mia then brought in some hot **COCOA** and pastries for all of them.

Soon, they all made plans to go on a short tour in and around Chennai for there was still time for the school to start.

~ ☀ ~

SCARED

By Vandana Gupta

Six-year-old Deepak returned home from school, threw his bag on the sofa and jumped onto his **BED**.

Usually Deepak would come home, would **run** around the house, talk about what happened in the bus, at classes, lunch break, and everywhere in school. He would not sit down even for a minute. In fact, his mom would tell him to be quiet.

A Silent Cry

His mom looked at the quiet Deepak, touched his forehead and asked, "Deepu, how are you feeling?"

Deepak nodded.

"Has someone said something to you? Did you have a fight with someone?" Deepak shook his head side-to-side, which meant 'no.'

"Then get up, change your clothes and eat something," said mom, taking out his lunch box from his bag. She opened the

LUNCH BOX and said, "You haven't even eaten your tiffin!"

She again sat down beside him and asked affectionately, "Tell me, Deepu! What's the matter?"

But Deepak did not reply. He kept lying down and went to sleep. In the evening, when Deepak woke up, his mom said, "I've made your **FAVOURITE** snack, along with chocolate milkshake. Come and have them!"

Deepak walked out of the bedroom, but did not say or eat

anything.

"What is the matter, Deepu? Neither are you saying anything, nor eating anything!" chided his mom.

Deepak, now started crying. *He's been bothered about something since the past five or six days. He doesn't eat properly or go to play. And, he hasn't* **eaten** *anything since morning today*, thought Deepak's mom.

She then remembered Nilu, who studied in Deepak's class and was his friend. The kids ate and played together. She quickly called Nilu on her phone and spoke to her.

Deepak's mom listened, while Nilu spoke to her. But, she could not hold back her smile, after a while.

Tooth No More

Smiling, she went to Deepak and said, "So that's what has been bothering you! You lost a tooth!"

Deepak looked alarmed as though he had done something wrong.

"Don't be scared! You lost a **milk** tooth. It's supposed to fall. And, in its place a new one grows!" explained his mom.

"So I'll get a new tooth?" asked Deepu.

"Very soon! And it's not just you. Every child your age loses their **TEETH**, which are called milk teeth. I too, did lose my teeth, when I was your age," said his mom.

"But mom, blood came out too," said Deepak.

"When the tooth falls, sometimes it bleeds a little. That is very common."

His mother explained further, "At six months of age, a baby starts growing their first teeth. Slowly, they grow twenty milk teeth. When they become five or six years old, their milk teeth fall and new permanent teeth grow in their place."

A Teethy Explanation

"Why don't we get the permanent teeth right at the beginning?" asked Deepak.

"Babies, are small and **FRAGILE**, and their food is very soft. Their mouths don't have enough space. Later when our jaws strengthen, and we start having solid foods, permanent teeth grow. But why didn't you just tell me that you lost a tooth?"

"Well, you always tell me not to put any object inside my mouth. But, five days ago, I was chewing on a **pencil**. That's when one of my teeth started moving. So, I got scared. I thought you would scold me," replied Deepu.

"Putting objects in the mouth is an **unhealthy** habit, Deepu. Marbles, buttons, toys have harmful germs

and dirt on them. Sucking on them or putting them in your mouth, may give you stomach ache and infection. You **CHEWED** on the pencil and that's when your tooth started hurting. That's also when you stopped eating properly, and today, when your tooth fell, you got scared," explained mom.

"Yes, mom. I'm hungry, now! Let's eat those delicious snacks!" said Deepak.

"I hope my tooth will **GROW** again," said Deepak, while eating his favourite snacks.

"It sure will! But you too must make a promise. When you will lose your other teeth, you will not be scared and if you face any difficulty, you will not hide it from me. If you don't tell us, we won't be able to help you," said his mom.

With his mouth full of **delicious** food, Deepak nodded his head.

~ ☀ ~

FEEL IT RIGHT

PUZZLE TIME

In the following scenes, read the options and pick the right one.

If you're stressed before your exams, you will...
a. Sleep till you stop stressing
b. Set up your study space, finish studying and sleep on time
c. Watch video games

If you're nervous about talking on stage, you will...
a. Talk to a friend or family member
b. Make an excuse to skip the performance
c. Hide behind the curtain

If you fought with your best friend, you will...
a. Cry and never talk to him/her again
b. Get angry with everyone else
c. Talk to your best friend and try to find a solution

If you're anxious about your first day at a new school, you will...
a. Be rude so people are scared of you
b. Be quiet and avoid talking to anyone
c. Try to make new friends

If you lied to your parent and feel guilty about it, you will...
a. Confess and apologise
b. Hide your mistakes till you forget about it
c. Blame someone else for making you do it so you don't get into trouble

WHO STOLE MY TOOTH?

By Soumya Torvi

Rahil went running to his mother. "Amma, my tooth is shaking, please stick it back."

"I can't stick it back, my dear. It will fall soon and in its place, a new tooth will grow," said Ma. "No! I want this tooth only. If it falls, everyone in school will tease me," he cried.

"But, that will be only until your new tooth **GROWS** back dear," explained Ma. But Rahil wouldn't listen.

"You know, Soumil broke his tooth and everyone in school calls him, 'Gateway of India'." He burst out crying.

Seeing him cry, Ma promised to get him an ice cream in the evening and Rahil went back to play. But as days passed, his tooth started shaking more.

"You should eat jalebis, everyday. The gum in the jalebis will make your tooth stick back," said his best friend, Roshan.

Now, Rahil ate **jalebis** every evening with his grandpa. His baby brother would crawl up asking for a bite. "You can't eat without teeth, brother. Don't worry! We will eat lots of jalebis when you grow up," said Rahil kindly to him.

The lost tooth

One night, when Rahil was asleep, his little brother kicked him on the mouth in his sleep. "Ah!" Rahil screamed, his eyes still closed.

The next morning when he went to brush his teeth, he was shocked to see an empty space between his shiny teeth, staring back at him through the mirror. "No!" he shouted and Ma came running to him.

"What happened, Rahil?" she asked. "My tooth! Someone stole it Ma," he said.

"But why would anyone **steal** it, dear. It may have fallen off and a new one will soon grow in its place," said Ma.

But he wouldn't listen. "I don't want to go to school today," he cried. Seeing him sobbing, his mother allowed him to take the day off.

"Who could have **STOLEN** my tooth?" Rahil wondered, sitting outside. "I have to **SOLVE** this case," he thought and put on his police cap. "It couldn't be mom, as she has all her teeth in place. It can't be dad because he is out of town."

"I got it!" he said and ran to the bedroom where his mother was knitting. His brother was sleeping in the cradle. He went quietly to the cradle. "Don't wake him up," said Ma. "No, Ma. I just want to **CUDDLE** him," said Rahil and quietly opened Kunal's mouth with his finger and looked inside. His brother woke up and started c r y i n g l o u d l y. Before

his mother could shout at him, he dashed out of the room.

Where could it go?

"He doesn't have a single tooth. So, it couldn't be him. Then, could it be..." he thought and ran to the dining room where his grandpa was **READING** the newspaper.

"Grandpa, how many teeth do you have?" asked Rahil **ANGRILY** with his hands on his hips. "I had 32, but now I am left with..." grandpa said, trying to think. "Count them yourself," he said and opened his mouth wide.

"One, two, three, four..." Rahil began to count. "I knew it! It is you, who stole my tooth," said Rahil.

"Really? But, why would I?" asked grandpa.

"So that you can eat **CHIKKI** like me," said Rahil. "I know you like them."

Grandpa thought for a moment and asked, "What colour was your tooth, dear?"

"It was sparkling **WHITE**," said Rahil proudly.

"But all my teeth are yellow or brown. Check for yourself," said grandpa and opened his mouth wide, again. Rahil peeped inside his grandfather's mouth and saw his teeth.

"They are so dirty, grandpa! Don't you **brush** your teeth twice everyday like I do?" he asked.

"I do," replied grandpa. "But my teeth are old like me."

The many remedies

Rahil broke into **TEARS** and showed grandpa his mouth. "Everyone at school will make fun of me," he cried.

Grandpa thought for a minute and said, "I have an **IDEA**!" he beamed. Rahil wiped his tears and grandpa went to the bathroom and returned with a packet of white powder.

"Take this, rub your teeth with it and gargle every morning," he said. "What is this, grandpa?" asked Rahil. "It is tooth seed," replied grandpa. "When you rub it on your gums and gargle with it, it plants a new tooth."

Rahil remembered his grandfather's gardening lessons. He was excited to wait for a new tooth to grow in his mouth. **GRANDPA** gave him another packet and said, "These are LEMON candies.

When you go to school, distribute these candies to your friends and tell them that whoever makes fun of your fallen tooth won't get any." Rahil was satisfied.

Next day, he went to school merrily. No one made fun of him as they wanted the tasty lemon candies. A few weeks passed by with Rahil rubbing the white powder on his mouth and gargling everyday with it.

Suddenly, a new tooth sprang up in the empty space between his teeth. He was excited and told grandpa that the seed had grown into a tooth.

Grandpa grinned and thought, 'My tooth powder SAVED the day!'

~ ~

SAKSHAM'S WRAPS

By Rajkumar Dhar Dwivedi

"Hey Saksham, why don't you come over to my house?" asked Kanchu after playing cricket in the morning.

"I'm sorry Kanchu, I don't think I can. I need to go home quickly," said the ten year old Saksham.

"But it's a holiday today. What are you going to do at home?" asked Kanchu.

"My **PARENTS** are not in town and I have to go make breakfast for my grandfather."

"What? You can cook?" asked a surprised Kanchu.

"A little bit," said Saksham. "My mom taught me."

"Wow! Then in that case I'm coming with you. I can't wait to try your cooking," said Kanchu.

"Great! You can help me **cook** too," said Saksham.

"Sure, but I can't even boil water properly so I'm not sure how much help I will be," said Kanchu and started laughing. Saksham laughed too.

The two made their way to Saksham's house where his grandfather was reading the newspaper.

Saksham's Surprise

"Grandpa, have you had anything to eat yet?" asked Saksham.

"No son," said grandpa. "I just came back from the **HOTEL** after having some tea. Here is some money, why don't you go get us some breakfast from the hotel?"

"No need for that grandpa," said Saksham. "I'll go make some potato wraps for you."

Grandpa **SMILED** and offered to help but Saksham politely refused and told him that if he would call him if he needed any help. Grandpa asked him to be careful and got back to his paper.

Saksham and Kanchu entered the kitchen. Saksham picked up some potatoes, washed them and put them in the pressure COOKER  with a little water. He carefully lit the gas and put the pressure cooker on the stove.

"Give me some work," said Kanchu. "I'll have something to do and I'll learn how to cook in the process."

"Alright, why don't you pull out the FLOUR and knead some dough," said Saksham. "Take the flour in a bowl, add some water and mix them."

"I'll give it a try," said Kanchu.

The two got back to their tasks. Saksham turned off the gas and took the pressure cooker off the stove. He took out the potatoes and let them cool down. Then he began to peel the potatoes. When he was about to mash them, Kanchu had finished k n e a d i n g the dough. Saksham took a look and couldn't hold

his laughter in.

"Oh Kanchu, should I call this DOUGH🌮 or porridge? There is so much water here," said Saksham. "Why don't you mash the potatoes? In the meantime, I'll fix the dough."

Once Saksham was done fixing the dough, he began working on the filling. He lit the gas and put some ghee in the wok. Once it was hot, he added some JEERA and some chillies. Then, he added the potatoes and let it cook. Soon, the filling was ready and Saksham turned off the gas.

A chef in the making

It was now time to make the *rotis* for the wrap. Saksham tore off small chunks from the dough and began to flatten them with the rolling pin. He lit the gas and placed a *tava* on the stove. He spread some ghee on the surface of the tava and placed the *roti* on it. When it was cooked on one side, he flipped it over. When all the rotis were cooked, he turned off the gas.

Saksham placed the filling in the middle of the *roti*. He added some ketchup and some mayonnaise and rolled up the *roti*. The wrap was done.

Saksham and Kanchu served the wraps to grandpa. He took a bite and loved them. He was all in praise of Saksham's cooking.

As Saksham, Kanchu and grandpa sat together to eat the wraps, Saksham's parents arrived. When grandpa told them that Saksham had prepared breakfast and

how yummy it was, they were pleasantly surprised.

"I was so worried about what you were going to have for breakfast," said Saksham's mother.

"Enough about us, have you two had breakfast?" asked Saksham.

"No, we haven't. I was planning on making breakfast for all of us. But I guess I will have to cook only for your father and myself."

"No need, we have made enough for everybody," said Saksham.

Saksham's parents asked him what he wanted as a reward.

"The fact that you loved my cooking is my reward," said Saksham.

Saksham's parents gave him a big and they sat together and ate Saksham's wraps.

~ ❋ ~

COLOUR ME

WHERE ARE MY GLASSES?

By Sonali Garge

Kannu and Mannu had just woken up when they heard their neighbour, Prakash uncle call out to them, "Children, come here to help me find my glasses. I can't find them."

"Okay, uncle. We are coming," they said together. They quickly brushed their TEETH and ran over to Prakash uncle's house to look for his glasses.

Prakash uncle often **misplaced** his glasses and could not recall where he had kept them. And whenever that happened, which was often, he called Kannu and Mannu to help him.

They looked everywhere. On the table, near the window, on

the fridge, in the kitchen, on the television and even in the backyard but couldn't find the glasses.

The search

Prakash uncle was **UPSET** as now he couldn't do anything without them. The children kept looking but had no luck.

Just then, Kannu and Mannu saw their neighbour, Jugnu pass. They called him and ran to the door to tell him about Prakash uncle's glasses. "Uncle lost his glasses again. I don't understand how this happens every time.

He is so smart otherwise. He remembers everybody's phone numbers, **addresses** and names. He is good with maths too. Then how can such a smart person forget where he kept his glasses every day!" Kannu said, exasperatedly.

"Kannu, this generally happens with most old people. They can do different tasks with ease but lose track of small things. The famous **scientist** and inventor, Thomas Alva Edison was known for overlooking small things," said Jugnu.

"A long time ago, Edison was working on a project in his laboratory. His cat and her kittens lived with him in the **laboratory** too. They kept leaving the room and coming back. He had to leave his work and open and close the door for them whenever they wished. This disturbed Edison. So, he drilled two holes in the wall—a big one for the cat and

a small one for the kittens. Now, the cat and her kittens could easily come and go without DISTURBING him."

An important story

"EDISON then got busy with his work. After a few days, he saw the cat and kittens use the same hole to come in and go out. He laughed at himself and said, 'why didn't it occur to me that the kittens and cat could use the same HOLE! What a fool I am to not think of this small thing! There was no need for me to make the small hole at all'."

Kannu and Mannu nodded when they heard this story. They couldn't believe that such a great mind could overlook such a small detail.

"Just like Edison didn't think of such a small thing, Prakash uncle, too, is busy with many tasks and **forgets** small things like where he has kept his glasses. Now, go to him and ask him when was the last time he used his glasses," said Jugnu.

"Alright, Jugnu. Let's go, Kannu," said Mannu.

An organised search

"Uncle, when was the last time you used your glasses and what were you doing then?" asked Mannu.

Prakash uncle thought for a while and said, "I was sitting right here, on this sofa, reading today's NEWSPAPER. Then, I went to have a bath."

"Ohh! Now, we know where they are. Just wait here, we will get

108

your

glasses," they said and ran to the bathroom and saw the glasses on the **shelf**.

Within seconds, they were back and handed the glasses to Prakash uncle. This time, they got a string and tied the glasses to them so that Prakash uncle could wear them around his **NECK** and not lose them again.

"**THANK YOU**, children," he said, seeing the string and got on with his work.

THE DARING TRIO

By Akiladeswari Sivaramakrishnan

Heena, Salim and Krupa, grade 7 students, were good friends. It was a strange **friendship** as Heena had recently joined the school and was studious whereas Salim and Krupa were known for their pranks.

Most of the classmates didn't like to hang out with Salim and Krupa as they kept getting into trouble.

Though the two never did anything to **HURT** anyone, their puckish attitude was not well-received and they would end up in trouble.

"I never wanted to steal your **bicycle**. I just wanted to make you go around searching for it."

"I was just playing with your hair. I don't know how they got entangled."

"We forgot our **TEXTBOOKS** hence, we took yours."

These were some of their common pranks. Even though Heena never joined them in their pranks, she enjoyed them thoroughly. She was also a victim of their pranks but knew they both were good at heart.

Their school **ANNUAL** day was around the corner. Heena, Salim and Krupa were participating in a singing competition and had to stay back after school for practice. Their parents were asked to pick them up once the practice was over.

An unfortunate incident

One day, heavy rain and thunderstorm lashed the city. Most of the students had gone home while Heena, Salim and Krupa were still at practice.

By the time practice got over, their parents couldn't come and pick them up as the roads could not be navigated. The school principal received a call from them and he asked the trio to stay back in school for the night till the

weather cleared out. They were given a classroom to sleep.

Krupa sat by the window watching the RAIN flood the streets.

Salim drew funny faces on the classroom board. Suddenly, he saw a shadow through the gap of the door. He peeped out and saw a few men walking through the corridor with some BAGS. Heena stood right behind him.

"What are these men doing in our school?" asked Heena.

"I don't know. Look, they are ENTERING the other classroom," replied Salim.

Krupa joined their conversation and suggested that they alert the SECURITY guards. She went to the window and tried to call out to the security guard when she noticed something shocking.

"Salim, Heena, look here. The security guard was just given a bundle of notes by that man. Probably, he too belongs to that gang in the next room. This looks CREEPY, guys," said Krupa.

Investigation Continues

"I will go and eavesdrop the conversation in the next classroom. You two stay here and tell me if you see anyone else entering the school," said Salim as he stepped

out of the class.

He walked towards the classroom where the men were and hid below the glass WINDOW in the corridor. He peeped and saw that the men stood in a CIRCLE and were talking.

After some time, he saw the men remove some powdered packets from the bags and hide them in a vault inside the brick wall in the classroom. Once done, they covered the vault by placing the BRICKS back in their original position.

Salim went back to tell Heena and Krupa.

"What! We need to stop this," said Krupa. Heena nodded.

"Why don't we trap them here and call the principal?" asked Krupa.

"What do you mean?" countered Salim.

Krupa explained the plan to both of them.

She walked to the other classroom where the men were and latched the door from outside.

The men heard her footsteps and tried to open the door but couldn't. Krupa quickly ran back to Salim and Heena.

Heena said, "I called the **PRINCIPAL** and told him what we saw. He is calling the nearest police station and they will be here soon."

Result of a smart plan

The trio stood outside the classroom and kept a watch on the other room where the men were trapped. The men kept pushing the door but it didn't open.

Soon, the sound of the **POLICE SIREN** filled the air. The policemen along with the principal opened the locked classroom and handcuffed the men.

"Sir, these men have hidden some powder packets behind that wall," Salim announced.

"Yes, sir. The security guard is also involved. We saw him taking money from these men," said Heena.

"Drugs!" said the startled principal.

"Thank you so much, children, for capturing them inside the premises till we arrived," said the senior police officer. Their principal thanked them too and PRAISED them for their bravery.

The next day in school, their story became popular.

From that year, they were recognised for their BRAVERY and became the talk of the town.

~ ☀ ~

THE PALACE OF WINDS

By Poonam Mehta

It was *Summer* and the temperatures were high. Twins, Sona and Mona were visiting their grandparents in Rajasthan. Their grandparents lived in Jaipur, the capital city.

They saw the desert for the first time on the way. But Jaipur was green and not full of **SAND**! The heat was sweltering, of course. Their grandma was overjoyed to meet them.

Grandma was not keeping well, but now she felt better. She said that seeing them had improved her health. Sona and Mona spent most of their time with their grandma.

One day, the weather became extremely hot, and there was a power **FAILURE**. Even the inverter in Grandma's house ran out of battery within a few hours.

There was no fan and no light inside the house. Sona and Mona who lived in the hills were finding this heat unbearable.

Beating the heat

"It's so hot, grandma! How did people survive in the olden days when there were no **fans**?" asked Sona, irritated with the heat.

Mona nodded and said, "They must have not been able to do anything."

Grandma smiled and said, "It was never this hot in olden days. It's getting hotter and hotter now because of increased **POLLUTION** and population."

"But still, how could they live inside houses in such weather? Today we have air conditioners, but there weren't any in those days," they said together.

Grandma thought for a while and then said, "Get ready! We'll go somewhere!"

The girls were overjoyed to hear this. They were getting bored and restless sitting at home without electricity.

Grandpa took out the car from the garage and Mom, Dad, Grandma, Grandpa, Sona, and Mona—all set off for the **City Palace**. Through the window of the car they could see the pink gates, pink buildings, green Jaipur, the hustle bustle, people in **COLOURFUL** dresses. Sona and Mona were enjoying themselves. The City Palace was magnificent.

A Breezy Trip

Grandpa bought tickets to the Hawa Mahal or the Palace of the Winds.

Grandma said, "We should have come here in the **MORNING**."

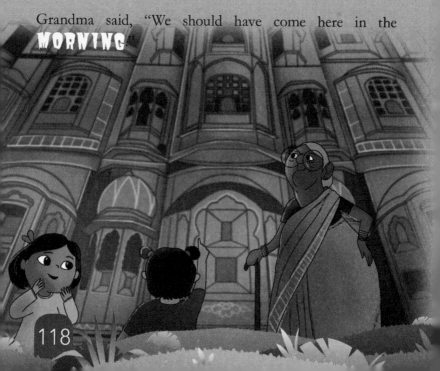

118

"Why?" asked Sona and Mona.

"When the morning sunlight enters the palace, it looks **beautiful**. It's a sight to behold," said Ma remembering visiting it as a child. She too was seeing the Hawa Mahal after many years.

Grandpa hired a guide, who told them that the Hawa Mahal was built in 1799 by Maharaja Sawai Pratap Singh. He was the **GRANDSON** of Maharaja Sawai Jai Singh, who was the founder of Jaipur.

The city palace was inspired by the Khetri Mahal in Jhunjhunu, which was constructed by Maharaj Bhopal Singh.

As Sona and Mona walked through the palace, the guide described the monument. Hawa Mahal was five-storied and it did not have any **staircase**. People had to use the ramps to reach the floors. It had 953 small windows or jharokhas, and small rooms from where the street could be observed.

Sona and Mona asked, "Why so many windows?"

The guide said, "It was meant for the **ROYAL** women to observe everyday life and see the festivals celebrated in the street below without being seen. They had to obey the strict rules of the 'purdah' system, which forbade them to appear in public without covering their faces."

"Lal Chand Ustad was the architect of this unique structure," said the guide.

He showed them the interior designs and said, "The architecture reflects a fusion of Islamic Mughal architecture and Hindu Rajput ARCHITECTURE, evident from the floral patterns, fluted pillars, domed canopies and arches."

The beautiful structure

The Hawa Mahal was built like a honeycomb with small portholes. Each porthole had miniature windows and carved sandstone grills, finials, and domes. Sona and Mona were engrossed in the beauty of the architecture. Ma and grandma looked at the market below through the JHAROKHAS.

Sona looked at the stone slab and rubbed it.

The guide smiled and said, "That's pink sandstone. It does not fade. It stays cool during summers and warm during winters. It does not crack easily so the palace was built with this stone."

"But this is not a palace!" said Sona. "Why then is it called 'Hawa Mahal'?"

"The fifth floor was called the Hawa Mandir and thus it got the name 'Hawa Mahal'," said Grandpa. "Also this palace is built right at the centre of the market. From outside it looks just like a honeycomb. The air entering through the

jharokhas cools down the insides, and so it started being called the Hawa Mahal."

Indeed, Sona and Mona did not feel hot at all while they were inside the palace. They were enjoying the cool wind.

Both were excited about seeing the Hawa Mahal. They were impressed how in the olden days, people found a way to BEAT the weather, safeguard the privacy of women, and create an architectural wonder.

The Hawa Mahal was a POPULAR tourist spot in Rajasthan. And they were glad to have seen it.

~ ~

COLOUR ME

THE SLIPPERY TONGUE

By Omprakash Kshatriya

Bacto was fast asleep when suddenly his tongue asked, "Do you know me?"

Bacto laughed and said, "Who doesn't know you? You are my tongue!"

"You are absolutely right, Bacto!" replied the tongue. "But I am sure you don't know that I am a muscle. Although I have a name, but I am really a muscle of your body."

"Yes, I didn't know that you are a muscle," said Bacto.

The tongue continued, "I am the STRONGEST muscle of your body. Though I am attached from only one side, I work tirelessly. Once I start, no one can stop me. I leave everyone behind. The teeth that you see around me are very strong."

"If I continue wagging I can bring people up to breaking these too. I stay comfortably within the strong teeth.

However, sometimes I get bitten by them causing **INJURY** to me, but I heal very fast too," the tongue went on.

"Self-praise is not good. It is not an attractive **habit**," Bacto retorted.

The tongue was aware of this phrase. It went in and said, "Oh, yes! I forgot I was telling you about muscles and I started to praise myself. This is called self-obsession."

The Knowledgeable Tongue

"Let that be. Do you know your body is made up of 600 types of **MUSCLES**? They help you move and give energy to your body. Very few people know that they cannot survive without muscles in their bodies," the tongue continued.

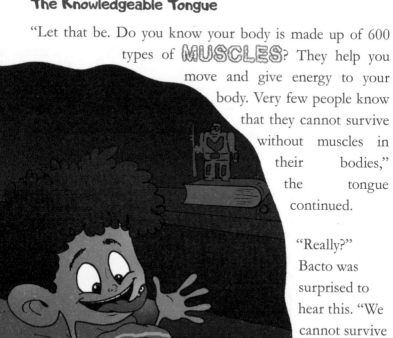

"Really?" Bacto was surprised to hear this. "We cannot survive without muscles!" he repeated, his eyes open in astonishment.

"Yes. Your **HEART** and lungs are made up of muscles too. It is these muscles that pump blood in your body and help you to breathe. If it were not for them, you would be dead long ago," the tongue explained.

"Your face can express emotions of happiness because of muscles. If muscles stop working you will not be able to smile, even. They play an important role when you CRY as well. You are able to write because of hand muscles. In other words, muscles play an important role in everything you do."

"Does that mean that we can do things that we like to do only because of the muscles in our body?"

Muscle Mania

"Oh, no," the tongue was quick to add. "There are some muscles that work on their own. They do not need any instructions from your mind and are called involuntary muscles. Like your heart beating or your LUNGS breathing, happen on their own and are not controlled by your mind."

"Some muscles are controlled by the mind. Like when you are thinking about something or asking a question. These actions are controlled by your mind that give instructions to the muscles that perform that action and therefore, are called

voluntary muscles. You have control over these."

The tongue wanted to c o n t i n u e further but the T E E T H were not pleased. "Talking so much is not very pleasant," they said.

But the tongue wouldn't stop. It could not stop, once it started talking. That is why it is said that the tongue can't hold itself.

"Stop it now," warned the teeth, but the tongue did not pay any heed and continued blabbering. This **IRRITATED** the teeth and they bit into the tongue. The tongue was hurt and finally it became quiet.

Bacto was fast asleep when this happened. He woke up in **pain**. His tongue was hurting. He drew his tongue out of his mouth. He had bitten himself while **sleeping**.

Bacto was happy as he had a wonderful **dream**.

~ ~

THE ALIEN FRIEND

By Smita Dhruv

Vicky was **curious** about everything connected with space, including extraterrestrial creatures or aliens.

Vicky's mother encouraged him to read science fiction stories and let his **imagination** run free.

Vicky listened attentively whenever his mother told him stories about all the scientists who were involved in space research.

Vicky's school had a Science Club with children across ages as members. Today, their Science teacher had shown them a film on spaceships and alien theory.

Vicky came home very **excited** in the evening. "Mummy, do you know there are extra terrestrial beings floating in the sky? Many people have seen aliens with their own eyes!"

Today he had learnt a lot about *aliens* and the things they could do. Vicky was convinced that aliens were stronger and more powerful compared to human beings.

Sadly, Vicky's excitement was not shared by his mother. She smiled, but also looked a little disturbed.

Vicky hugged her. "Why are you upset mom?" he asked.

"The servant who comes to do the house work has not turned up since last week. I'm not sure how I'm going to be able to take care of my work at the office and take care of the house."

A Weird Encounter

Vicky felt **SAD** when he heard mother's words. "How can I find someone to help Mom?" he thought.

He did not talk to anyone at home afterwards. He did not go out to play with his friends either. Instead, he finished **DINNER** and went off to sleep early.

As soon as Vicky went off to sleep, he started dreaming about space and aliens.

It was almost **midnight** when he woke up with a start. He felt that someone had entered his room through the window.

Vicky was scared. He tried to open his eyes with some effort, and in a **blurred** vision saw a figure standing over his bed.

Vicky woke up with a start and sat up in his bed.

Looking intently at the figure, Vicky realised that the figure was not **HUMAN**. He had a heavy body and bald head. His clothes looked like they were made up of some kind of plastic. It had a lot of switches and lights attached to it and were flashing constantly.

The SHINE from the suit illuminated the entire room. Vicky was excited. He knew that this can be none other than the Alien that his teacher had described.

Vicky meets an Alien

Vicky jumped out of bed, and went near the TALL figure. "Who are you?" Vicky asked.

The tall figure bowed respectfully, and said, "*Ummm Rictosop.*"

"Wow! What a wonderful name. I finally have an alien friend of my own." Vicky started clapping happily.

"Tomorrow I will take Rictosop to the SCHOOL, and the whole class would be impressed to see him." thought Vicky.

Then he remembered something. His mother needed a helper for the house. "Maybe Rictosop can help," Vicky said to himself. "Let me take a test first."

"Rictosop, can you move my bed from the ground to the CEILING?"

Rictosop again bowed to Vicky, and in fraction of a second Vicky found his cot hanging in the air. Vicky was impressed.

"Rictosop, can you please get the cot back to the ground?" The command was followed and Vicky's cot was back in its normal place.

Vicky decided to use his alien friend to solve his mother's problem. "Rictosop, can you finish all the house work that my MOTHER has to do tomorrow? She has to reach office on time."

A Quick Helper

Of course, this was hardly any work for Rictosop. He immediately went to the **kitchen** and moved his head from right to left and lo and behold, the kitchen became sparkling clean.

All the **utensils** had been washed, dried and placed properly. The table has been cleared, clothes folded and preparations for the next morning's breakfast were made too.

"Wow! Mom will be so HAPPY," Vicky said to himself.

He decided to hide Rictosop for some time under his bed before announcing his arrival to the rest of his family.

As he tried to throw the **blanket** over Rictosop, somebody pulled the blanket away and shouted, "Wake up Vicky! Time for school!"

Vicky opened his eyes. There was no **RICTOSOP** anywhere to be seen.

His mother was standing in front of him. Vicky looked at his mother and realised that she looked happy today.

"It can't be," said Vicky and jumped out of bed. He rushed to the kitchen and it was just as clean as he remembered.

A few minutes later, he heard his mother speaking to his dad, "Good that Gopal came last night. All my work is done, and now I can go to work without any worry."

Vicky was SAD. After all, it was not Rictosop, but Gopal who had done the work.

~ ~

SCALE A MOUNTAIN

Here's your chance to climb atop a mountain. Solve the math problems starting from the bottom to reach the top.

6. 10x10 + 20/ 2

5. 16/8 + 12 – 10

4. 9/ 3 + 8 x 7

3. 12 x 5 / 2

2. 8/ 8 x 4

1. (5+3) X 8 + 1

* Answers on the last page.

BRAVE ANITA

By Dr K. Rani

Aman and Anita were ready for SCHOOL. Their mother, Rama, quickly put bread and milk on the table. They had their breakfast quickly and left for school with their bags.

"Aman! Hold Anita's hand and walk carefully," Mom advised.

"All right, Mom!"

"You're her elder brother. You're supposed to take care of her."

Aman grabbed Anita's hand and started walking. Rama told Aman the same thing everyday when they left for school.

They both studied in a primary school in the village and went to school together.

Aman was in the fifth standard and Anita was in the fourth. Rama kept reminding him that he was a boy and that he was an elder brother.

The Lake

Anita was a restless and fearless girl. She would actively participate in all kinds of activities at school.

There was a small lake on their way to school. The L A K E had a narrow, rickety bridge, which the villagers would use.

Even the schoolchildren crossed the lake using it. However, when they reached the lake today, the bridge was filled with water, which usually happened when it rained.

"The lake's filled with water. How will we cross it? Let's go back home," said Aman.

"No, bhaiya! Our teachers will be annoyed. Let's walk a little ahead and cross the lake using the other bridge."

"What bridge? It's an old tree, which fell down years ago. How will we walk on it?"

Crossing Over

"The other villagers are using it. We should too."

"But I'm SCARED."

"Bhaiya! There's nothing to be scared of. We'll hold ☐∩∩☐○ and walk over that tree," said Anita encouraging him.

They walked to the tree, which the other villagers were using to cross the lake. Aman was still afraid.

Anita grabbed his hand and said, "We'll cross the lake safely, don't worry!"

Aman slowly got on to the tree and somehow managed to cross the lake. He heaved a sigh of relief when he reached the other side.

"Did you see that, Anita? I crossed the lake!"

"Of course, you're so brave!" said Anita and they went to school.

The other **children** from the village had also managed to reach the school. By afternoon, the water level had receded and they returned home via the usual way.

Rama was waiting for them. "There you are, kids!"

"Did you know that the lake was full of water this morning? I grabbed Anita's hand and crossed the lake by walking on the tree-bridge. Right, Anita?"

"Of course, you did," lied Anita.

"Your brother is really brave, Anita. He's fearless," Rama praised her son.

"I'm fearless too, Mom," said Anita.

"Girls aren't fearless at all. They're always scared and take their brothers' help to do everything. You crossed the lake today because Aman helped you," said Rama.

Anita did not respond.

A week passed. It hardly RAINED and the lake did not fill up again. They walked to school as usual.

A Terrifying Incident

One day, on their way back from school, as they were about to cross the lake, Anita heard some noise from the bushes nearby.

She said, "Wait, bhaiya! There's something in the bushes."

"What?"

"I think an **animal** is hiding there." Anita looked carefully and saw the tail of a leopard peeking out of the bushes.

"Look! You can see the tail of a leopard among the bushes. It's waiting for a prey."

Aman was terrified and was about run, but Anita grabbed his hand.

"Where are you going, bhaiya?" she whispered.

"It's a leopard! It'll attack us!" said Aman.

"If we run away, the leopard will chase us. Let's wait here for sometime."

"I'm so scared!"

"I'm scared too, bhaiya. Look, our **friends** from school are also coming this way. We have to stop them."

"We'll stop them as we run," suggested Aman.

"We may stop and save them, but this leopard can attack all of us. Even if we get saved, it could attack someone else."

"I don't understand! I'm going back!" said Aman and quietly walked away.

"Wait, bhaiya!"Anita followed him. They met their friends and said, "A leopard is hiding in the bushes ahead."

"We can't run away," said Anita.

"Why not? We should save ourselves," said Sohan.

"We should also **save** others' lives if we can. Let's wait here. If we see someone approaching, we'll stop them so that the leopard doesn't attack them," said Anita.

"We're scared."

"Why should we be scared? There are so many of us. Let's pick up **stones**. If the leopard comes out of the **BUSHES**, we'll scare him, but make sure not to harm him for no reason," said Anita.

The others agreed. They picked up stones and held on to them.

They kept an eye on the leopard from afar. It was still waiting for someone to come closer. None of them took a step forward.

Suddenly, their teacher came behind them. He asked, "Why are you all standing here?"

Sohan explained everything.

"We can't go that way. We'll go home through some other way," said Aman.

"But we need to do something about the LEOPARD or someone will get attacked."

An act of bravery

"Anita's right! We have to scare the leopard off. We

shouldn't run away. If we just find another way to go home, the leopard will attack someone else," said their teacher.

Everyone agreed. The teacher took a stick in his hand and walked ahead. Anita walked right behind him and the others followed her sheepishly.

Their teacher said, "Throw the stones near the bush and scream all at once. The leopard will run away hearing the commotion."

The children threw stones near the bush and screamed together. The leopard came out of its hiding and seeing the crowd, it ran away into the jungle. They all finally breathed a sigh of relief.

The teacher said, "Anita, you're a brave girl."

"Sir, you are the one who taught us that we shouldn't run away from problems. We should face them," said Anita.

They reached home late that day. Anita did not say anything. It was Aman who PRAISED her today.

"Mom! You should've been there!"

"What happened?" asked Mom and Aman narrated the whole story. He told her how Anita stopped them from running and how they all drove the leopard away.

"And it was Anita who did all this?" asked Mom surprised.

"Yes, Mom! I was scared. I couldn't even speak. But she wasn't at all."

Rama Anita and said, "You're a brave girl, indeed. You've done what others were too scared to do."

~ ☀ ~

FAST-FOOD PROBLEMS

By Dr Amitabh Shankar Rai Chowdhury

When Nina returned from school, it was time for her daily **TANTRUM**. Kanti, the cook, had prepared rotis, dal and carrots with capsicums like always.

Nina made a face and shouted, "I don't want to EAT this!"

Ma tried really hard to get her to understand that eating fast-food everyday was not healthy. It could harm the liver and cause obesity.

Nina didn't listen and called her dad on his mobile phone. "Daddy, I want you to get me a Chicken **pizza**  and a burger immediately. I will not eat this roti and dal."

And what would her dad do? Being his only daughter, he would spoil her and give in to her every demand. When he returned home in the evening, Nina's dad had picked up the burger and the pizza on the way. Nina jumped at the burger and finished it off in minutes.

Wasting Food

The food Kanti had kept in the casserole remained untouched as Nina ate the pizza for dinner.

"Is something wrong madam?" she asked Nina's mom. "I had prepared the ROTIS keeping in count how many everybody eats. Why is there so much left over?"

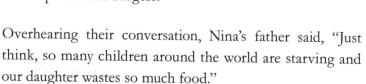

"What do I say? Nina refuses to eat the FOOD that is cooked at home. The only things she will eat are pizzas and burgers."

Overhearing their conversation, Nina's father said, "Just think, so many children around the world are starving and our daughter wastes so much food."

Kanti asked if she could pack the leftovers and take them home.

When it was time for Nina to go to school, she said, "Kanti, no need to prepare food for me. I'll be eating at the school canteen," and went to school.

When it was time to eat, Nina used the money her mother had given her to buy some **CHIPS**  and a cold drink. As soon as she opened the packet in front of her classmates, they jumped at her and ate all the chips. All she was left with was the cold drink.

When she was coming back home in the school bus, her tummy started grumbling and began to hurt. She was running a **FEVER** too.

Sick and unhealthy

When she reached home, both her parents were still at work and Kanti was the only one there. When she called up her dad, he told her that he wouldn't be able to come home early. He suggested that she take Kanti and visit their family doctor.

When they reached the clinic, the doctor took a closer look. When he checked her stomach, he said, "There's some swelling here, what did you eat last night?"

145

When Nina told him, he began scolding her.

"Only fast-food 🥤🍔?" he said. "The only thing you can get from eating fast-food is fat. What did you have for lunch?"

When she told him, he shouted at Kanti as well. "A child is spoilt only by her parents. When her parents get home, tell them to make her eat the food cooked at home and not to buy her junk food all the time. Apply a hot water **BOTTLE** to her stomach and she should be fine."

When they stepped out of the clinic, bid drops of water came crashing down from the sky as well has Nina's eyes. It began raining.

"My house is nearby," said Kanti. "We won't be able to travel far in the **rain**. Why don't you relax there until your father picks you up?" she suggested.

They quickly bought the medicines the doctor had prescribed and went to Kanti's home. When her children saw Nina, they became very excited.

"Nina's feeling unwell. She will stay with us until her father comes to pick her up so don't trouble her," Kanti said.

Good food craving

Nina-*didi*, the food mummy had brought from your house was so yummy. We had that for lunch today. We are fine, how come you're **unwell**?" they asked.

Nina felt bad that Kanti's children were so happy that they got to eat the **LEFTOVERS** from her house. She felt even worse for only eating fast-foods all the time.

"How are you feeling, Nina?" asked Kanti. "If you're feeling better, you could ask your daddy to come pick you up."

"Kanti bua?" asked Nina with respect. "Do you have any food left over? I'm feeling terribly hungry."

Kanti bua was surprised to her words. "Oh my poor baby," she said. "I'll go get you something right away."

When she came back with the food, Nina took the PLATE with a big smile on her face.

"The food prepared at home is prepared with **love**," said Kanti bua. "You will never find that special ingredient in the food that comes from a restaurant."

Nina understood the importance of eating HOME COOKED food and rarely ate fast-food.

~ ☼ ~

SPOT THE DIFFERENCE

PUZZLE TIME

Circle 10 differences you can find between the two pictures.

THE BOY WHO HOPES

By Lekshmi Gopinathan

The cold breeze envelops the sleepy valley of Srinagar. The pine trees with mountain peaks in the background look picture perfect. Hassan sits at his window, staring at the stillness.

The CALENDAR flutters on the wall and Hassan looks at the date. It's August 15. This is going to be the second year that Hassan hasn't stepped out to celebrate Independence Day at school. In fact, he can't remember the last time he stepped outside. Everywhere he turns, he hears the words lockdown and coronavirus.

Over the past year, he has also learnt that lockdowns in Kashmir aren't new. When the lockdown was announced all over India because of the virus, Kashmir had already been under one for months.

Sneaking out to meet Ali and Imran was strictly not allowed by Abba and Ammi. Ammi's phone had rung only once or

twice over the past couple of months and then there was silence again. The internet connection started and stopped without any notice.

He thinks of the last time he had **HALWA**, yummy delicious halwa. Everything was rationed. This Ramzan, he didn't get any new clothes, but Hassan understands that clothes are not important. Things were changing; he was growing up.

Following Rules

"Hassan, I am headed to Rukhsar aunty's home." Ammi's warm voice reaches him from the kitchen.

"Ammi, I want to go with you." Hassan pleads. He hasn't been to the bazaar or anywhere in a long time.

Ammi looks at Hassan and lets out a deep sigh. She, too, only went to the market, following rules and ensuring everyone's safety, but looking at Hassan's face she said, "Okay, go put on your mask and wear the **full-sleeved** shirt."

Hassan throws his arms around his lovely Ammi who is frail, thinner than before.

Hassan skips along Dal Lake as he looks around. During summer, Dal Lake usually had the world-renowned floating market, with shikaras floating on the lake carrying flowers, vegetables and people. This year, Dal Lake is deserted. He wonders if this was how Srinagar would always be.

Hassan breathes in the cool **MOUNTAIN** air and feels his lungs opening. "Ammi, why are we going to Rukhsar aunty's?" he asked.

"She offered to give us some vegetables from her garden,

Hassan," replied Ammi.

Hassan looks around and spots a makeshift stall full of **bright**, red and juicy tomatoes. He tugs at Ammi's sleeves. Ammi shakes her head and leads him on.

Hassan looks at Ammi and questions, "Why have Abba and you been eating less?"

Ammi swallows a lump in her throat and turns to Hassan. "We don't have work right now, beta. We are just saving some **MONEY**."

"Will you always have to eat **LESS**, Ammi? Is it this virus? Will you never be able to go back to work? Will the bazaar never open again?" Hassan asks questions that have kept him wondering for days now.

"The times are a little different, Hassan." Ammi lovingly touches his face.

"Why are times always different for us?" Hassan almost screams.

He looks around and sees the shops with their shutters down. The tour and ticketing shop run by Uncle Akhil is shut. The photo studio run by his friend Imran's abba, where he and his friends went to get their school identity card photograph clicked, is empty. The **BIG BUILDING**, which had people with heads bent on computers looked haunted by ghosts.

He looks at the small number of people rushing to their destinations, silently. Once upon a time, each one on the street had a mobile and would be talking loudly. Was that just a year ago? Everything feels like a distant MEMORY and that scares Hassan.

The questions continue

"Why don't we still have proper phone connections, Ammi? Will it always be like this? Will we always stay disconnected? When can I go back to school and write my exams, Ammi?" Hassan's young voice is pained with his questions.

Hassan can see Ammi's eyes flood up from behind the mask. Taking a deep breath, she BRAVES the cold wind and turns to Hassan.

"Hassan, we live on hope, on UMEED. That's the only thing that keeps us going. We will continue to believe that one day Kashmir will be back to normalcy and so will be this world."

Hassan hugs his mother tight and both make their way to Rukhsar's house. The only sound that accompanies the shuffle of their footsteps is the distant sound of the army patrol and the whistle of the wind.

Aunty Rukhsar is Ammi's close friend. They used to work together with carpet weaving artisans.

"Alia, Hassan. I was waiting for you." Rukhsar looks at them with eyes full of love but maintains distance. Hassan feels that warm hugs were also exchanged a lifetime ago.

"Here you go. I hope they are enough to get you through the season." Rukhsar hands over a big bag of green vegetables to Ammi. Hassan sees **cabbages**, haak and green peppers in the overstuffed bag. With quick goodbyes and nods, Ammi and Hassan walk back home.

"What will we have for **dinner**  today, Ammi?" Hassan asks as soon as they step inside their house.

Ammi smiles and adds, "Haak, we will have a yummy, filling and nutritious meal today."

Once home, Hassan changes into his **kurta** and pyjamas

and puts on a thin woollen pullover. He steps into the warm kitchen where Ammi is picking out the green leaves.

Hassan and Ammi cook

"Ammi, what's special about haak?" Hassan asks, seeing Ammi clean delicate and tender leaves and stalks.

"Haak is a food of respect, most of the leaves used would be thrown out otherwise, but for this dish, we use all of them. It's called a **poor man's meal**. The ones we are using today is Kaatchie Dal Haak."

Hassan watches as Ammi heats mustard oil in the pan. The sputtering and simmering remind Hassan of firecrackers.

"Are we poor, Ammi?" Hassan asks quietly. He knew the past one year had been the **toughest** in his ten years.

"Why do you ask, Hassan?"

"We are eating a poor man's meal, Ammi."

Ammi smiles at Hassan and adds asafoetida and dried, long **RED CHILLIES** into the pan.

"Hassan, the times are tough and while Abbu and I do not have **JOBS**, at the moment, we are still doing better than so many other people around us. So, can we call ourselves poor?"

Hassan thinks of the stories he has been hearing over the months about people dying, both because of the virus and otherwise.

Ammi switches off the flame, adds water, then switches it back on and adds the haak to the boiling mix. The kitchen is filled with a tangy **fragrance**. Hassan feels his eyes smarting but enjoys the feeling.

Ammi crushes some green chillies and adds them, covering the simmering greens and letting them cook slowly.

"**AACHHOOO**!" Hassan sneezes in response. Both of them burst into laughter.

Mouth-watering!

Ammi switches off the stove and adds some salt. Hassan's mouth waters. Laughing, Ammi ladles out a huge bowl of **RICE** and puts haak right in the middle.

Handing it over to Hassan, she waits as Hassan tastes the simple Kashmiri haak and rice.

"Ammi, this tastes magical," Hassan grins as he gulps the entire bowl.

Ammi laughs, "See Hassan, we got something NUTRITIOUS and simple out of what we would have been throwing into the dustbin."

"Ammi, I want to go back to school and lead a NORMAL life. I want to go back to playing with my friends. I want to go back to a year ago."

Ammi stands speechless as Hassan spells out his wishes and looks out of the window at the starkness of the city, holding his bowl of rice close. He can smell despair and sorrow.

Four SEASONS have passed but in his little heart, he still hopes for better news. That he will go back to learning lessons, playing games and most of all, living normally like other children of his age. Hassan hopes that he will again get a chance to celebrate August 15 at school in Kashmir.

ANSWERS

PUZZLE TIME

Page 12: Maze

Page 26: Map Quest

Zeba went to Egypt, Tanzania and Madagascar.

Page 51: Sequence

Page 133: Scale A Mountain

1. 65
2. 4
3. 30
4. 77
5. 4
6. 60